Claire Still Kicking

Claire
Still Kicking

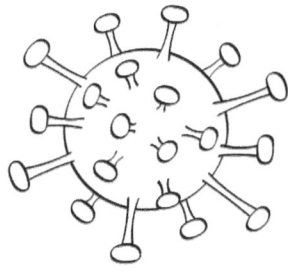

**Stories and Poems
from the
COVID Pandemic**

by Rose Baldwin

SENESCERE

Yucca Valley, California

Published in 2023
Printed in the United States of America

ISBN 978-0-9981390-4-3
SENESCERE. Yucca Valley, California

Table of Contents

The Pandemic Starts ---------------------- 7

Retirement Community Pool ----------- 15

Sheltering in Place ---------------------- 16

Tea Time --------------------------------- 25

Sewing Bags ----------------------------- 27

Condo Watchdog ------------------------ 37

Community Involvement --------------- 39

Kaboom ---------------------------------- 48

Neighbors -------------------------------- 50

The Next Step --------------------------- 66

An Ambulance Comes ------------------ 67

Age Warriors ---------------------------- 76

Stanley Returns ------------------------- 77

If --- 91

Ronnie Meets a Fella -------------------- 92

Desert Seasons-1 ----------------------- 100

Snowbirds Return ---------------------- 102

Desert Seasons-2 ----------------------- 108

Restless ---------------------------------- 110

The Pandemic Starts

Everyone is talking about COVID, taking note of its spread, but few people have made any significant changes to their daily habits. Claire and her friend Ronnie have invited their newest friend Phyllis to join them in making the short walk from their retirement community to their favorite bar for happy hour. They expect to have a small meal and a large glass of wine. Respectful of admonitions to practice social distancing, upon arrival, they arrange themselves farther apart than usual, even though the distance combined with their faded hearing will make conversation tricky.

It's only after they're seated that Claire notices the usual day-drinkers aren't there. They're alone. "Hey, we're the only ones here," she says. "Where's Chuck?"

Chuck the bartender knows what the women want. Sometimes he gives them oversized drinks. They like him.

Staring at the television mounted behind the bar, Ronnie says, "Shhh... the governor's making an announcement. He's ordering all the bars to close. Can he do that?"

Claire and Phyllis think Ronnie has misunderstood and turn to help her watch. The story is repeated and then commented on. Businesses are being told to shutdown to reduce the spread of COVID.

"Oh my god!" Claire says.

"Can they do that?" Ronnie asks again.

"It's like something out of a movie," Phyllis says.

The women sit watching one narrator then another repeat or comment on the story and their wonderment increases. They accept the seriousness of the virus, and understand the need for precautions, but closing the bars strikes them as...well, unbelievable.

Chuck walks out of the kitchen. "Hello ladies," he says. "We've been ordered to close. I'm saving what food I can and getting rid of perishables. I'm sorry but I don't have any wine open. Would you mind having martinis instead? I make a good one."

The women, distracted by a new announcer on the television, each in their own way, indicate assent. They only turn back to Chuck when he places the drinks in front of them.

The first to take a sip, Phyllis, says, "Wow, this is a good martini."

"I love the little bits of ice floating in it," Claire says.

"I didn't know you could get olives with blue cheese in them," Ronnie says. "I love blue cheese."

"Remember, they're stronger than wine. Sip," Chuck admonishes, while giving each of them a glass of water. "Water is for thirst."

The women nod.

Chuck goes back into the kitchen and returns a few minutes later carrying a tray, loaded with nuts, chips, veggies and cheese, that he puts in front of them. "We were expecting a

group this evening but that was cancelled because of the virus. I hate to
see this go to waste."

The women snack heartily. But
even with the food to absorb the alcohol, they're acting loose and happy
by the time they finish their drinks.

"You know, Chuck," Claire says,
"there isn't much vodka left in that
bottle. I bet you could just make a
couple more drinks and finish it off."

Ronnie's grin is mischievous.
"And, you know, since vodka has
more alcohol than wine, it might
even kill COVID, right? We're in the
vulnerable age group, you could be
saving our lives."

Chuck smiles. "You're walking?"

The women nod.

"Okay, but I need to be sure
you're steady enough to make it
home."

For a moment there's confusion about how they might demonstrate steadiness, then Claire says, "Yoga."

Chuck watches wide-eyed as they form a line and walk straight and sure onto the dance floor. Phyllis leads, calling out, "Mountain," and the women stand straight with their arms at their sides. "Volcano," and they extend their arms over head. "One leg." Phyllis and Claire stand on their left leg putting their right foot on the inside of the left knee, Ronnie does the opposite—as is her habit. "Switch," and they change sides.

"Okay," Chuck says. "But if you feel even a little unsteady, let me know, I'll drive you home."

"I knew that yoga class would come in handy," Claire whispers to Phyllis.

Claire is right about the vodka too, there is just enough in the bottle for three martinis. Their conversation becomes raucous with the woman expressing their shared political opinions, heavily peppered with expletives they usually avoid saying out loud and rude comments about politicians they dislike. At one point, they laugh so hard, all three have to run to the restroom.

After they finish their drinks and most of the snacks on the tray, Chuck checks again that they were steady enough to walk home. This time Ronnie leads them to the dance floor, and they repeat their routine. Their execution is better than most would expect from seventy-something-year-olds, and outstanding considering they've had two martinis.

As they gather their things to leave, Chuck hands each of them a to-go bag. "That group was also having dinner. I don't want this food to go to waste," he says. Then he wraps up the few remaining blue cheese stuffed olives and gives them to Ronnie. "See you gals when this is over. Take care of yourselves."

"You too, Chuck. See you soon," they say, not quite in unison.

They walk home having no idea how long it will be before the bar reopens and how many things will change in the meantime.

Retirement Community Pool

Billy and Bobby Johnson
may have been well built once
but now they are a frightful sight
in their swimming trunks

Fronts are dominated
by each man's enormous gut
and in the back their cracks show
framed by withered butts

But they are not self-conscious
their strut shows they are proud
as if those cracks and bellies
were made to thrill a crowd

Sheltering in Place

As alarm grows over the spread of COVID, tourists flee the popular California desert resort towns around Palm Springs where Claire and her friends live. Among the first to go are the Canadians who dash for the border after receiving notice that their travel health-insurance is being cancelled. The immune-compromised also leave, wanting to be home, near their family doctor—in case. Some snowbirds stay a bit longer, either because they doubt the seriousness of the virus or they are intent on getting their money's worth out of the trip, even if it kills them. But after the entertainment venues close, they soon tire of the need to amuse themselves and go home. Until, at last, it's only full-time residents who are left behind, gleeful at the prospect of a spring without seasonal people.

Claire is determined to make the most of this time and sets up a writing schedule, but the words won't come. Then she tries rearranging a closet but loses interest. The news, with its constant reports about COVID's progress, is a powerful distraction.

Normally Claire and her friends would be going to a class or lecture at the senior center, or to a movie. They like movies and have premium cable channels, plus Netflix and Amazon Prime but watching at home isn't the same as seeing them on a big screen, and the popcorn doesn't taste as good.

When Ronnie shows up at her door with a picnic basket and an invitation to join her for lunch, Claire gladly accepts.

Ronnie arranges their food on one of the outdoor tables.

"I can't stay home this much," she says.

Thank goodness for Ronnie, Claire thinks, taking a bottle of carbonated apple juice out of the basket and pouring them each a glass.

"I was going to bring some vodka but I don't remember where I put my flask and the liter bottle didn't fit in the basket," Ronnie says.

"I keep my flask in the emergency preparedness kit under my bed," Claire says.

"Now that you mention it, I think that may be where I put mine. People laugh about it but vodka can be used to keep water tanks fresh, clean wounds and of course, fight depression—every emergency preparedness kit should have some."

"Yeah," Claire says. "It's also nice to have a little stash in case you run out."

While they eat, they talk about how hard it is to find masks. Ronnie says a local service organization is looking for people to sew them. She has a bunch of fabric she'd like to use up and plans to volunteer. Claire envisions the bins full of fabric she has and agrees to volunteer with her.

They're disappointed when they receive a box containing the materials the organization wants them to use—their own fabric will continue to take up space. *Oh well,* Claire thinks, *it's still a worthwhile project.*

Sewing should provide a distraction but somehow Claire can't escape the news. She turns the TV on to listen to the rock'n roll station, included in her cable package, then switches to the news—just for an update—but gets hooked and never switches back.

When their community pool and gym close, Claire and Ronnie start walking in the morning for exercise. They wave to neighbors who sit on their patios, in their pajamas, hair uncombed, drinking iced coffee—a level of casualness the seasonal people consider unacceptable.

Some mornings Phyllis walks too regaling them with stories about the challenges she's facing redecorating her recently purchased condo. She tells them she's certain the man she bought it from hadn't updated anything in the fifteen years since his wife died. His furniture, dishes, and kitchen utensils were left in the unit —a fairly common practice in the area. While this meant Phyllis was able to move right in, it also left it up to her to sort through someone else's things. Disposal of the unwanted, but still usable, stuff is complicated by the closure of the resale stores that accept donations. Phyllis is not someone who throws still-useful things away, so she makes room in her second bedroom for the "to be donated" items.

The kindest thing that can be said about her furniture is it is serviceable. Everything is out of date and needs a good cleaning, at least. Most pieces need refinishing. Fabric has to be covered or replaced. The pandemic doesn't distract Phyllis from her project; the home improvement stores are open, Amazon delivers, and handymen are working.

By the time Claire and Ronnie stop sewing masks because of the shortage of elastic, commercial masks are available, and Phyllis has a living space she's eager to show off.

During their morning walk, she says, "Come over about four. I'll show you what I've done. It's only the first phase but I think it's a good start."

Claire and Ronnie were skeptical about Phyllis's decorating ideas. But, seeing her house, both admit it looks terrific. She's painted the worn and dated wooden furniture in bright colors, some with designs, and then recovered the seats. She made or purchased slipcovers for upholstered pieces. The effect is to turn homely old junk into pieces of art.

The walls have been painted in various shades of white, making the rooms look larger. The carpet has been removed and laminate flooring installed over the concrete, making the floors softer and easier on aging hips and knees.

The women move to her patio where a tray with cheese and savory pastries is set up. Phyllis accepts their compliments while she pours a small amount of brown liquid out of an ornate pot into equally ornate, though unmatched, demitasse cups.

"Ohhhhhh, it's whiskey!" Ronnie says, after taking a whiff. "I thought it was going to be tea."

"Bourbon," Phyllis says. "My father taught me to appreciate it. This virus has me a little blue. I think it's time to take up light drinking and I don't want anyone talking about us."

"Works for me," Claire says.

"Yeah, me too," Ronnie says.

The women sit companionably watching their neighbors take evening strolls. Some who pass are people they saw drinking coffee this morning. The women speculate about what was in their cups.

Tea Time

We sit on the front porch
my good friends and me
sipping bourbon out of cups
that were made for tea

Char and Doris sashay by
they both dress like teens
Agnes strolls by with a beau
making sure that they are seen

Poor ol' Tom he had a stroke
but he won't let it keep him down
he plants his walker before each step
he's a hero in this town

Orange-haired Anna walks 'n waves
our resident beauty queen
Joyce walks fast with her new hip
looking fit and lean

But Joyce is not the quickest
though her pace is hard to beat
it's Charlie with his power chair
who's the fastest in the fleet

We provide an audience
my good friends and me
sipping bourbon out of cups
that were made for tea

Sewing Bags

During its weekly Zoom meeting, the leader of Claire's meditation group mentions that a nearby emergency food distribution center is running out of bags and asking people who sew to make and donate reusable cloth ones. Ever hopeful of using up their accumulated fabric, Claire and Ronnie volunteer. They decide to work together at Ronnie's, she has a multi-leaved dining table they can use as a work space.

Taking a break from remodeling, Phyllis joins them bringing her sewing machine and a bin with her.

"Fabric?" Ronnie says, waving toward the bin.

"Yes. I keep buying it thinking I'll make something, then, I don't. I'm hoping we can use some for the bags."

"We know," Claire says pointing to two bins already stacked next to the table.

Inside Phyllis's bin is an impressive stack of fabrics with sale tags. She's a careful shopper. There are also folded flat items with Goodwill and other resale store tags on them. Claire considers herself a good bargain hunter but has to admit that Phyllis may have her beat. She is drawn to some drapes in the bin.

"Aren't they beautiful?" Phyllis says. "There's enough to cover a twelve foot span. I got them for $3 at the Salvation Army resale store. Only one panel is sunburned. I have much more fabric. This is my smallest bin."

"So do we," Claire and Ronnie say together.

The volunteers were given a pattern for the bags the distribution center expected, but none of the women want to mess with the bound edge it calls for. So instead, they dig through Ronnie's stash of cloth grocery bags and find one about the same size but much easier to make and use it as their pattern.

"Think they'll object?" Ronnie says.

"If they do we'll take the bags somewhere else. Or maybe set up a booth at the next craft fair and sell them," Claire says. "If that fails, we can give them to one of the charity resale stores."

Ronnie and Phyllis chat while setting up their machines. "Phyllis, we've been so busy with all this COVID stuff and your remodel we hardly know anything about you. What's your story?"

"You know I'm from Chicago. I worked for an insurance company and retired five years ago. I lost my partner, Dorothy, to cancer three years ago. We were best friends for over fifty years. I met her in high school."

Dorothy?! Her!? Claire wonders what else she's missed. Maybe Ronnie was right when she told her to have her hearing checked.

Claire's sewing machine is easy to set up, and she has a piece of fabric the right size for a test bag so she's ready to start sewing before the others. She puts her head down and begins, still fretting about her hearing. She doesn't want to wear hearing aids. If people would just speak up, she could hear just fine.

"We shared a room in college and then just kept living together after school," Phyllis says. "When it became legal, we were going to marry but Dorothy got sick. We were afraid her bills would bankrupt me—as a friend/roommate I had no financial responsibility and she qualified for additional services."

"It's like me!" Ronnie says. "Not the cancer part, but I met my husband, Todd, when we were in high school. Oh, my god! This is the first time in your life you don't have a partner. That's just like me, too. Listen, it gets easier. Now I understand the story you wrote for the memoir class about wanting to jump off that building. It was just like that for me when Todd died. Then I moved here. There are a lot of widows here. There's a grief group at the seniors center. Oh, wait, that's all closed. Well, come talk to me."

Claire listens while she works. She can hear them just fine.

"How long have you been alone?" Phyllis says.

"Oh, gee, it's almost ten years. The time sure does fly."

"Have you tried dating?"

"I've thought about it. But I haven't met anyone who attracted me," Ronnie says. "Are you thinking you'll try to meet someone?"

"I don't know. I've never been with anyone but Dorothy, that way, you know."

The bag Claire is working on is easier to make than she'd expected. She's already half done.

"Yeah, Todd was the love of my life," Ronnie says. "He visits me at night just as I'm falling asleep. We cuddle. He tells me that he hates to see me alone. That I should make an effort to meet someone."

"Dorothy visits most nights and says that same to me. But I can't actually picture who I could meet. I never had to date and didn't know how hard it is. You know, things are different now, especially around here. For most of our lives Dorothy and I hid our true relationship. We always said we were roommates.

"The last few years before she died we sorta' came out. But we were so used to hiding the truth, it felt odd, we never got used to it. We liked being in Palm Springs and walking down the street holding hands. That never felt quite right in Chicago. I don't know how to..."

"Flirt?" Ronnie says.

"Yeah!"

"It's the same for me. I saw one fella I thought was handsome and thought about, you know, flirting, but I didn't know how. Turned out it was a good thing. A little while later I heard he swindled a woman he dated. I can't afford that. It's hard. No one I meet is near as nice as Todd."

Turning to Claire, Ronnie says, "You're awfully quiet over there."

Claire doesn't want to talk about how much she misses her dead husband, how alone she feels, how much worse the pandemic has made it. She was taught not to talk about her troubles and afraid if she did she'd cry. So she changes the subject by holding up the bag she's been working on.

"I think this design is nice, fast, and easy to make. All it needs is handles," she says.

"Wow, this is great," Phyllis says, examining the bag.

"Yeah," Ronnie says. "They're so fast, we'll be able to make a bunch of them."

"Show us what you did," Phyllis says.

"Here, I have this stuff that we can use for handles," Ronnie says holding up some webbing.

"Remember to make them long enough to go over your shoulder," Phyllis says.

The women enter bag production mode. For some time, they are distracted from the pandemic and their personal woes. They use up a lot of fabric, and the food distribution center likes their bags. The ones made from the drapes Phyllis got at the Salvation Army store are everyone's favorite.

Condo Watchdog

People avoided Ron Carson
when he strolled down the walk
he never shared a happy word
though he sure did like to talk

the fees we pay aren't fair
the board's a bunch of crooks
reserves have been misused
they're treating us like schnooks

No one took him seriously
all those complaints he roared
about the righteous volunteers
who were serving on the board

But when the treasurer died
the truth came out at last
Ron Carson had been right!
the board held a wicked cast

You'd think they'd hide their faces
but in that you would be wrong
they stood and shouted back
we've served you all along!

No one wanted to admit
they'd been duped and cheated
so the scoundrels stayed in place
and the good guys soon retreated

The truth would hurt home prices
so why create a fuss?
those who cared, just moved away
abandoning the muss

Community Involvement

"I'm thinking of volunteering for our condo's security committee," Phyllis tells Ronnie and Claire during a late afternoon cocktail hour on Claire's second floor patio.

The women laugh.

"What?" Phyllis says.

"Oh, I don't think you have the patience," Claire says.

"Claire's being polite," Ronnie says. "You're way too logical and smart for any of the committees."

"But we just had that theft," Phyllis says. "Maybe I can help prevent another."

Claire and Ronnie exchange a look.

"We need to tell you some of the things the security committee has done, then you can decide if you want to join," Claire says. "I'll start with the security codes on the entry gate because it's easy to understand.

"There used to only be one code to open the gate. It wasn't changed for years at a time and what with the delivery people, realtors, and repair people, half the town knew it."

"Yeah," Ronnie says. "Then there were a couple thefts, and so, finally, the code was changed. But then, a bunch of the owners complained. A woman who couldn't remember the new code wrote it next to the keypad with a black marker."

"So," Claire resumes, "after many discussions, the committee decided that there should be different codes, the owners would have one and deliveries, contractors, and realtors would each have their own. It was a good idea. The codes for service providers could be changed periodically increasing security and owner code would stay the same."

Ronnie fidgets with frustration and then interrupts. "But then no one changed those other codes. None of them have been changed in three years! We're right back where we started!"

"Maybe the intent wasn't made clear to whoever changes the codes," Phyllis says. "That can happen."

Ronnie stares at her. "Phyllis, you're a kind person. I'm guessing you'll lose your patience when you've been here a longer."

Claire continues. "A while after that we had another string of small thefts, mostly just taking stuff that was lying around unprotected."

"Can you believe people leave their wallets in unlocked cars, in wide-open carports?" Ronnie says. "Well, anyway, that's what they said. Sorry to keep interrupting, Claire. I get riled up every time I think about this stuff."

Claire smiles and takes up where she left off. "The thieves came into the community by cutting the chain link fence by the dog park."

"And do you know what the committee did?" Ronnie says. "They changed the front entry. Whenever vagrants climbed or cut, that fence by the dog park—that's all the way in the back of the property, as far as you can get from the front gate—the committee reinforced the front entry. That's why we have the separate entry gate for pedestrians, the cameras, and those nasty spikes that scare me every time I drive over them."

"And," Claire says, "each one of those safety improvements, individually, cost the community more than the total of everything broken or taken by intruders."

"That doesn't make sense," Phyllis says. "Was anything ever done to reinforce the back fence?"

"No, people still come through there all the time," Ronnie says. "Our maintenance crew patches the cut places."

Phyllis looks skeptical. "Listening to you, the committee members sound a little dim," she says.

"Oh, but there's more," Claire says, "and this is my personal favorite. There were two women who didn't want their unit number on their carport parking space. One thought it was a safety issue, the other one had two lovers and hoped to confuse them about whether she was home or not."

"As if they wouldn't recognize her car," Ronnie says.

"Anyway," Claire says, "the two of them kept insisting that the numbers be changed so the parking space number wasn't the same as the number of the unit it belonged to. It was such a minor thing, no one thought about it. We all figured the committee would pick a starting place and number consecutively from there. But that's not what they did."

Claire sighs.

Ronnie takes over. "You know the office keeps a set of keys for each unit so they can get in if no one sees you for a while and they need to do a wellness check, or for some other emergency."

Phyllis nods.

"Well," Ronnie says. "A code was developed so that the number on the key held in the office would be different from the unit number. That way if anyone broke into the office, they'd have a hard time figuring out what key opened what unit. It was a good idea. But then the security committee used that code for parking spaces and sent a copy of it to everyone."

Phyllis inhales loudly. "That reduces the security of the keys," she says. "And the randomness of the numbers on the parking spaces is confusing and just plain odd."

Ronnie shakes her head. "That's why the spaces in my carport are numbered 3349, then 5720, then 6394, then 5559. It's ridiculous."

Claire and Ronnie admire the sunset while Phyllis sits quietly looking down at her hands.

After a while, Phyllis says, "Yeah, you're right. That sort of silliness would drive me nuts. Maybe I'll join one of the other committees."

"Maybe," Ronnie says. "Maybe not. Every one of them has a story."

"For years the finance committee refused to issue any financial statements," Claire says. "When they finally did, they weren't accurate. The grounds committee spends thousands of dollars every year planting annuals instead of getting perennials. It goes on and on. And, even when people volunteer to help, the existing board and their minions find ways to block them."

Phyllis sighs. "You're right I hate shenanigans like that. I guess the only hope is that since entry through the back of the property prompted them to reinforce the front gate, maybe the fact that the most recent robbers came in through the front gate means they'll fix the rear fence."

Claire and Ronnie nod. "We can only hope," they say, then raise their glasses in a toast.

"To our board and their mischief," Ronnie says.

At other happy hours Ronnie and Claire tell Phyllis more stories about the board. When a building collapses in Florida, Phyllis has an opportunity to watch their board in action. It isn't a pretty sight.

Kaboom

When that building in Florida
collapsed on to the ground
condo boards everywhere
took time to look around

were there pipes, or plugs, or studs
failing at their location?
was there work they had not done
that might lead to ruination?

but our board was well practiced
in neglectful governance
they only worried they might be sued
and knew not to take that chance

the first and only thing they did
and they did it without shame
was to increase the insurance
that shielded them from blame

Neighbors

"This COVID thing is getting worse and worse. We're all seniors, the most vulnerable group. We need to meet the rest of the people here in the complex," Claire says. "Just waving at one another isn't enough."

Ronnie shakes her head and says. "What are you suggesting? We can't have a party, gatherings aren't allowed because of COVID."

"With this virus spreading we need to make sure everyone has someone checking on them. We have to watch out for each other," Claire says. "I think most people here have connections but that one couple seems isolated. I'm going to go introduce myself to them. Wanna come?"

Ronnie and Phyllis demur.

The couple keeps very much to themselves. Counter to the area norm, they travel in the winter and return for the summer—the pandemic has grounded them. Claire and the others see them walking around the complex in the evening. They respond to greetings, but they never stop to talk. The women have been told they are strange.

"Good luck," Ronnie and Phyllis say.

The next morning Claire walks to the couple's unit at the far end of the community, inhales deeply, and rings the doorbell. The wife, Maudine, opens the door almost immediately.

"What a nice surprise," she says. "I just made a pot of coffee. Come in. Come in."

Her face looks freshly scrubbed and moisturized. Her hair is tied back with a scrunchie. She is barefoot. When she turns and walks into her house, her brightly-colored-silk caftan billows behind her.

Claire follows.

"You're Claire Wilson, right? The one who writes those clever poems," she says, without turning.

"Yes," Claire says to her back.

"It's so nice to finally meet you," Maudine says while moving around her kitchen, preparing a tray.

"I have orange scones," she says. "Let's sit on the patio then we don't need to wear masks."

This is not at all what Claire has prepared herself for.

"So, what brings you here?" Maudine says.

Maudine's busy energy and cordial reception has so confused Claire that it takes a few beats for her to remember what she came for.

"Well, um," she says. "I thought with the virus and all, that we should check in on each other and make sure everyone is all right and has everything they need."

"Aren't you just the sweetest thing?" Maudine says. "Would you like a little Irish in that coffee?"

Without waiting for a response, she gets the bottle from a nearby cabinet and adds the whiskey and then some cream to both cups.

She sets a cup in front of Claire, then settles into her seat and takes a generous swallow of her Irish coffee.

"I know the rumors," Maudine says. "People have been saying I'm strange for decades. I'm used to minding my own business, and don't much like the seasonal people. Maybe I am a bit strange."

She takes breath before continuing.

"My father died during my junior year of high school and then my fiancé was killed in Vietnam. I settled into what today would be called depression. For years I was a sad, sulking, silent presence working in the records department of the local school district. I probably could, even should, have gotten help, but admitting mental health issues was frowned on in rural Indiana, where

I'm from. Some silly people in town thought my suffering was romantic, a sign of my broken heart—stupid twits. When my mother sickened and needed care, the school administration offered me a very nice early retirement as an inducement to leave. No one hid their relief when I accepted it.

"It took a while, but Mother recovered enough for us to travel. River cruises were our favorite. Mom couldn't walk very far so I'd get a wheelchair and push her around the towns where we landed—unless there were cobblestones, then she'd stay on the boat, and I'd go ashore alone and tell her about the city when I got back."

Claire relaxes, she's enjoying Maudine's story.

"Mom was a clothes horse, she loved dressing up so we joined tours that offered formal meals and parties. The people we travelled with hadn't heard that I was strange. With them I was allowed to be just fine. Those trips became my primary social interaction.

"Then, my mother died, as they do. The few people who had visited when we were home were old friends of hers and they stopped coming around, leaving me to a solitary life. I felt as if I was invisible."

She pauses to take a bite of her scone, a drink and a deep breath.

"It wasn't that I hid. I went to the store and the library like everyone else. Sometimes I went to church, but no one ever seemed to notice me, and they certainly didn't strike up a conversation. I suppose I let my grooming slip a bit, but no worse than a lot of people. It got to the point that I doubted anyone but the lawyer who managed my financial affairs remembered I existed. Who was there to dress up for? It's not healthy to be that alone."

Claire thinks Maudine should have been on the stage.

"I knew I needed to do something. A famous general was coming to the country club on Memorial Day. He started his career in Vietnam in the same place my sweet, sweet fiancé, Billy, died. I thought attending the event could honor the past and mark the beginning of a fresh start.

"I was scared because I hadn't been to any events for quite a while and couldn't think what I'd say to people. Then I remembered that the conversations at such gatherings are fairly predictable. Someone would likely comment on how well the event had been organized. Someone else would say it was hard to get the general to come to our small town. All a person has to do is agree. Someone might ask if I was a member of the club and I'd tell them I wasn't, but my mother had been and I was considering it.

"I worried for days about what to wear and finally settled on my mother's pink Chanel suit—you can't go wrong with Chanel. I accessorized with her jewelry, including a dazzling ring she said gave her courage. Mother said that a ring like that let people know, whatever else they might think of you, you were not to be messed with. That you could make trouble. I tied my hair back and put on my glasses with the rhinestones in the frame, the ones I saved for good. I had my Chanel bag over my arm and was giving myself one final check in the mirror thinking, *Mother would have carried her Hermes bag but I like the Chanel*, when the doorbell rang."

Claire leans forward, curious about who was there.

"I opened it and saw a police officer. He looked sort of familiar, but I didn't know where from. He smiled as if he knew me. 'Maudine?' he said. 'It's me, Vance, from biology class. Please, I need to talk with you.'

"You can imagine my confusion. It had been decades since I'd graduated high school. How could I recognize someone who was in my biology class?

"'Vance?' I said. 'You got old, Vance. What happened?'

"'We all did Maudine,' he said, 'all but you. You look beautiful.'"

Claire watches as in that moment Maudine is transformed, looking years younger, a woman in love.

"Anyway," Maudine says, returning to the present. "He knew he shouldn't have said that and stood there acting awkward. Finally, he gathered himself, and said, 'I need to talk with you. May I come in?'

"I told him that it would need to be another time, that I was on my way to the country club to hear the general because he fought in the same place as Billy—Vance had known Billy.

"He told me that my neighbor had called the police chief and told him she thought I was up to no-good. That I'd been doing a lot of shooting. That she became concerned for the

General's safety when she saw my name on the list of attendees.

"I told him I had a squirrel problem and had been shooting them—or, shooting at them would be more the truth. I never was a good shot.

"He said the chief was close to retirement and wasn't taking any chances. So, just to be on the safe side, he'd sent Vance to sit with me for a couple hours and not to let me go to the country club.

"I was furious and yelled, 'The chief has you detaining me because someone told him they saw me shooting my old rifle on my own property?'"

Having lived in a rural community herself, Claire knew once someone was tagged as odd, people picked on them. She was furious right along with Maudine.

"He said he was sorry. I would have thrown a fit but he looked so sad I knew he was humiliated by what he was being told to do. I couldn't make it worse.

"So, since neither of us was going anywhere, I asked if he wanted some carrot cake and coffee. We added a little Irish, and talked. Turned out he'd lost his wife about two years earlier. A few nights later he took me to dinner. One thing led to another, and we became a couple and then married. I know it sounds silly but I wondered if Billy arranged the meeting—I always felt that he watched over me.

"My neighbor kept complaining about everything. Why do city people move to the country and then complain about all the country stuff? She didn't like the chickens, the chain link fence, or the metal tool shed. She wanted me to tear down the old horse barn. She hated when I shot at the damned squirrels. As much as I liked my old house, the constant complaints were wearing, and I was tired of those winters.

"My attorney told me he and his wife liked the Palm Springs area so Vance and I checked it out. When he retired we moved here.

"I sold my property to a developer who planned to build a subdivision. The bulldozers were pulling in as we were leaving. The neighbor came out of her house screaming. She'll have a hell of a time fighting with the developer, he's the mayor's son.

"Oh my, I've been chattering and didn't let you get a word in edge-wise. Have another scone. More coffee? We need to have another and then you can talk nonstop."

Without waiting for an answer, she gets up, and pours them each a second. Putting the refilled cup in front of Claire, she says, "Now, what's your story? Oh, wait, I've read the *Claire Stories.* I already know quite a bit about you."

Claire thinks Maudine might just keep talking, but she doesn't. She asks her what things she misses about home. The women talk about spring flowers, forsythia, tulips, daffodils, and lilacs. They have a lengthy discussion about hostas. Both women love peonies. They admit they miss snow, though not winter. Claire finds Maudine charming.

After that morning, Maudine and Vance, often stop to chat. Sometimes

they even join the women for a cocktail.

The Next Step

On our walk we see them
all nice and in a row
at the memory treatment home
sitting on the patio

As we pass we wave
some wave back and smile
we like to think we pleased them
if only for a while

We're worried we could be them
sitting on the patio
of a memory treatment home
all nice and in a row

An Ambulance Comes

The flashing lights of an ambulance at 2:00 a.m. wake those living in the vicinity. They don robes and slippers, grab flashlights and walk out to see who it's come for. They must have called those who live farther away, because even before the responders get their equipment into the house a group of near and distant neighbors is lined up to watch.

It's Roberta. The onlookers entertain themselves with speculation about what's happened. As usual, Frank takes bets. COVID is the crowd favorite followed by heart attack, then stroke.

When Claire walks out of Roberta's house pulling a wagon filled with pet supplies, topped by a yowling cat, Sally, in her carrier, and leading a reluctant dog, Harry, she can hear the crowd commenting about what her being there might mean.

I didn't know they were friends. Neither did I. She's taking the pets. That's not a good sign.

The gurney carrying Roberta follows. She's wearing an oxygen mask but is conscious and communicating with the EMTs. *It isn't COVID* a man opines, *they didn't put on hazmat suits.* Even though the commenter has no knowledge of protocols, his pronouncement disappoints. The onlookers know that if it isn't COVID it will be days before they find out what it is and are able to collect on their bets with Frank.

Roberta is put in the back of the ambulance and the doors close. Just as it is getting ready to pull away, a neighbor steps in front of the vehicle waves his arms to get the driver's attention and points at something behind it. The crowd follows his finger and sees Roberta's friend Louise, pushing her walker as fast as she can toward them, yelling and sobbing.

"Please, stop! Please. I have to say goodbye to my friend. Please, someone, stop them! Please. Please. Please." Her house coat is open and flying behind her.

Some can hear Roberta's matching cries of, "Stop. Stop." coming from inside the vehicle.

The ambulance backs up to where Louise stands panting and the rear doors are opened. Roberta removes the oxygen mask and the women call to each other.

"You are the best friend I ever had in my life."

"I love you more than my family."

"Come home if you can, I'll be waiting here for you. If not, I'll see you in heaven."

The EMTs indicate they must go. As the ambulance pulls away, someone goes to Louise, closes her house coat and ties it shut. Someone else rolls a wheelchair to where she teeters on the verge of collapse. She sits in the chair and cries body-wracking, chair-shaking, heart-wrenching sobs while her neighbor wheels her home.

Claire looks down at the leash and the wagon and sighs, imagining the chaos of introducing Harry and Sally to her two cats. What if Roberta doesn't come back? Oh well, Claire said she'd take care of them and she will, somehow. Feeling a hand on her arm, she turns to see Phyllis.

"I'll take them," her friend says. "Though, you'll need to show me what to do, I've never had a pet.

Two days later they learn Roberta had a small stroke, she'll recover but shouldn't live alone. Louise is relieved and delighted. She was told to move into a facility some months earlier but chose instead to stay near her friend. Now the two of them can move to a facility together.

Roberta's daughter joins forces with Louise's to somehow bypass COVID restrictions and arrange for their mothers to move into a brand-new facility. Roberta's only concern is for the well-being of Harry and Sally—they cannot come with her.

Claire assures Roberta her pets are doing well, that Phyllis has taken them and that she, Claire, is supervising their care. When Phyllis begins sending Roberta pictures of Harry and Sally sleeping in their new bed, lying in the sun, playing with their new ball, eating some fantastically expensive new food, Roberta lets Claire know her concerns are assuaged. She asks her to gently tell Phyllis that hour by hour photo updates aren't needed.

Claire delivers the message.

"I didn't want her to worry—they really are loves," Phyllis says. "I do wonder why the female pug is named Harry and the male siamese Sally. Do you know?"

Claire laughs realizing she should have told her sooner. "In 1993 Roberta took a pair of carriers, left over after the passing of her two cats, to the shelter with the intent donating them.

"But, at the shelter, she saw the original Harry and Sally in a shared a cage near the entrance. A placard explained the pair could not be separated. Since the shelter wasn't set up to house dogs and cats together, they were desperate to place them and waiving all adoption fees.

"Instead of just dropping off the carriers, Roberta adopted the pair. She assumed their names were from the movie *When Harry Met Sally*. Roberta said every time she called them to dinner she was reminded of the famous orgasm scene from the movie and thought to herself, *I'll have what she's having*. It made her smile, every time.

"When the original Harry died she went back to the shelter and found a seven-year-old female shitzu. She asked the dog if she would mind being called Harry. The dog wagged its tail which she took as acceptance. And so it was, as one or the other of the animals died, she would go to the shelter and get another, always one that was older and less adoptable. The dog was always named Harry and the cat Sally, no matter their gender."

At the sound of Harry pawing at the door, Phyllis jumps up and grabs

his leash, abruptly ending the conversation.

"Harry always goes for a walk at
this time," she says. "When we get
back he and Sally will have dinner.

Claire thinks Harry and Sally
have done an excellent job training
Phyllis and that her work here is
done.

Age Warriors

One by one our friends fall
in shock we watch them go
taken by a heart attack
or maybe it's a stroke

We know there's no escape
that we'll be going too
we don't know how or when
but it surely will be soon

We warriors hide our fear
struggling not to whine
bravely marching on
moving forward with the line

Stanley Returns

Even though Claire and her friends have each other for company and live in a place where they can enjoy outdoor activities, the COVID restrictions and limitations are getting on their nerves. The news that neighbor and friend Stanley will return from an extended stay with her sister gives them something to look forward to.

Claire is on the lookout for Stanley's battered Jeep, when she sees a white Chevrolet Suburban with pink polka dots drive past her house and watches to see where it goes. Her curiosity increases when it parks in front of Stanley's house. A woman who resembles her friend gets out, but it can't be her. The woman is dressed in girlie-girl clothes, has purple hair and is leading a standard poodle that's dyed pink. Stanley favors men's shirts and jeans, and wears her hair short and generally uncombed. She would never dress like this, never. And, she's a cat person.

Claire calls Ronnie. "There's a woman who looks like Stanley going into her house."

"Yay, Stanley's back."

"I don't think it's her. She's wearing pink slacks, and a floral top —with ruffles. She has purple hair cut in a bob, and a big pink poodle. She's driving a huge white Suburban with pink polka dots. Stan would never do that."

"Oh, you're right. That can't be her," Ronnie says. "I'll be right over. We can walk there together. Maybe it's her sister."

The woman who looks like Stanley is removing a dog bed from the Suburban when Claire and Ronnie get there.

"Hello. I'm Claire and this is Ronnie," Claire says, aligning herself so they can do an elbow bump.

When the woman turns, they are shocked to recognize their friend.

"Well, look at you," Claire says.

"Yes. Look at me," Stanley says. She reaches out and hugs her friends, in spite of pandemic prohibitions against such things.

While the three stand wrapped in their group hug, Phyllis arrives unnoticed.

"You must be Stanley," she says. "I've heard so much about you, I've been looking forward to meeting you."

As the women separate, Stanley's tear streaked face becomes visible to all.

Phyllis takes charge. "Did you just drive in?" she says to Stanley. "I bet you're stressed from being on the road."

She turns to Claire and Ronnie and says, "Come on girls, let's get this car unloaded. Then, we can go to my house. I have muffins and will make a fresh pot of tea."

Stanley tends to the poodle, setting out food, water and the bed, while the others carry her things into her house.

Finishing, Phyllis takes Stanley's arm. "Come, I'm Phyllis. I live two doors down—I bought Finger's place, you know, the cranky old man who drove too fast. I moved in around the time you left."

Ronnie and Claire walk behind them whispering to each other.

"What happened to her?" Claire says.

Ronnie shakes her head. "I can't imagine."

"Where's her Jeep?"

"Shhh...give her a chance to tell us."

"I like the purple hair," Claire says.

Ronnie nods. "So do I!"

At Phyllis's house, Claire and Ronnie sit on either side of Stanley.

"It's such a relief to be home," Stanley says. After a few sips of tea and bit of a muffin she is composed enough to tell them what happened.

"You know my sister had a stroke, and I went to help her. Then COVID hit. At first it was fine, we did her physical therapy in the house. As she recovered, we went outside into her screen room. My sister's favorite activity is shopping, so as soon as the stores opened, we went to the mall. She didn't want anyone to see her using a walker but loves shopping so much she relented.

"With her recovery going well, I started making plans to return here. My tenants had planned to be in my place for two or three months, four tops, while they looked for a place to buy. Poor things, both of them got real sick and then the real estate prices sky-rocketed—it took much longer than expected to recover from the virus and then find something they could afford."

"Why didn't you call?" Ronnie says.

"You could have stayed with me," Claire says.

"Thanks guys. I know you would've helped but our places aren't big enough for any of us plus a long-term houseguest to be quarantined. I wanted to come home to friends, not create a burden. I figured it would be over soon enough.

"My sister and I kept shopping. It was good exercise for her and fun for me, I so rarely do it. She's a lovely person, but we're very different. She's never been political, but she's in Florida and surrounded by Republicans. It was hard for me to hold my tongue around them. To be fair, they may have been restraining themselves around me.

"Anyway, one morning my sister told me she wanted to do something to show her appreciation for my help. She explained that she'd gotten rid of my clothes, and was taking me to get all new ones. She meant well. The joy she showed over coming up with this reward was so genuine I couldn't object. I just shut down and let her do what she wanted.

"So there I was wearing this stuff." Stanley looks down at herself. "My hair'd gotten fairly long. I thought we were going for a simple cut but the next thing I knew it'd been styled in a bob and colored purple. Then we got makeup! I don't wear makeup. But once I started I thought I looked washed out without it."

"I like the purple hair," Ronnie says.

"Thank you.

"Then, just as I was getting ready to leave, my poor old Jeep died. That truck-thing I drove up in came available. The previous owner had a party planning business. She met a vacationing Italian and went home with him, leaving a mess for her daughters to clean up. They were furious. When I went to look at the truck-thing I met Penny the Poodle. Who would abandon a pink poodle?

"From the first I felt as if we were kindred souls. Her roots were showing and she needed grooming. The daughters gave me a great deal on the truck-thing when I said I would also take Penny. I was the first person she'd let get near her. They said she growled and snapped at everyone else."

"I don't think I've ever heard a poodle growl and can't even imagine one snapping at someone," Claire says.

"Me either—especially a pink one. Anyway, they said she did it. When I took her for grooming I didn't mention that I wanted to let her hair go natural, so she got fresh color. It seems to make her happy, she prances as if she's on stage. And everyone who sees her smiles. We're going to keep it for a while."

Ronnie excuses herself then returns carrying shirts over her arm.

"These were my husband's. I kept them thinking I'd use them but never have. Can you use them?" she says handing them to Stanley.

Stanley holds one of the shirts up. "I love tuxedo shirts. They look great with jeans," she says.

"Oh, I have a some things, too!" Claire says. She leaves and returns with three plaid flannel shirts that had been her husband's.

"Perfect for cool evenings," Stanley says, accepting them.

Then Phyllis leaves and comes back carrying a tray with four fresh cups, a bowl of nuts, and a bottle of bourbon. Three pairs of jeans hang over her arm. She sets the tray down and holds up the pants. "Will these fit you?" she says.

Stanley goes straight for the label. "This is the brand I look for." Then she holds them up against herself. "Oh, yeah, these'll work."

"How can you tell by just holding them up?" Ronnie says.

"Oh, when you shop resale you get good at doing that," Stanley says. "Besides, I'm not all that picky."

"They belonged to my partner," Phyllis says. "I thought you looked to be about the same size."

Stanley's face softens. "Are you sure you're ready to part with them?"

Phyllis nods. "Yeah. It's time."

Stanley changes right there. The tuxedo shirt looks very good with the jeans. She ties one of the flannel shirts around her waist. The clothes suit her.

"Thank you, girls," she says. "I feel like myself."

Phyllis pours the bourbon and the women go onto the patio to watch their neighbors take their evening strolls and let them see that Stanley's back.

The details of what happens next change with each telling. The basics are that Vance and Maudine stop by. No one remembers who had the idea but Vance is dispatched to the beauty supply store. There he meets two young women who just got their hairdressing licenses. He brings them and supplies back with him.

The next morning the hairdressers are gone but everyone else is still at Phyllis's house, not because they drank too much but because as the evening got long they simply fell asleep. They wake to the smell of coffee.

Claire has pink hair, Ronnie's is blue, Phyllis's is green and Maudine's is bright yellow. Stanley's hair is still purple but has been cut short in the little-boy style she favors.

Vance's head has been shaved and a temporary tattoo applied—Claire vaguely remembers him saying he wanted to look tough.

At some point Penny, the pink poodle, was brought to Phyllis's house and lies sleeping next to Harry and Sally.

Vance walks out of the kitchen carrying a tray with mugs of coffee, and says, "Okay, a sip of coffee, some pet attention, and a quick freshen up. Then, we'll take my big old Cadillac convertible out, get breakfast, and show off our hairdos."

If

love knocked at my door
would I
recognize it as a long-absent friend
say hello
invite it into the sitting room
and serve tea and cake?

Not me!
I'd slam the door and yell
go away
you've hurt me enough
then eat the whole cake myself

Ronnie Meets a Fella

Stanley easily fits in with Claire, Ronnie, and Phyllis and joins them in their get-togethers. When Ronnie doesn't show up for cocktails, Phyllis and Stanley wonder aloud where she is. Claire fidgets.

"Oh, she asked me not to say anything. But I can't keep it to my-self. Please don't let on that you know," Claire says. "She has a date. She met him at the grocery store. They ate lunch at the deli. Then a few days later they went for a hike and now he's taking her to dinner. He's a retired engineer, something to do with city planning in LaCanada or maybe it was Pasadena, anyway, somewhere around there, maybe San Gabriel. That's all I know."

"How long do we give it?" Stanley says.

"Maybe she'll be lucky," Phyllis says. "I'll keep a good thought for her".

"I hope she doesn't get hurt," Claire says. "She's so easy going and doesn't have much experience. I'm worried he'll take advantage."

Ronnie is back to her regular routine in just over two weeks.

"I hope you had some fun," Stanley says.

"It was nice at the start," Ronnie says. "It was fun to be pursued. It was wonderful to be hugged. Then, I was feeling a little frisky. I made a simple dinner and took it and a bottle of wine over to his house. Do you know what he said? He told me I wasn't much of a cook."

"What did you make?" Claire says.

"The usual, clam linguine and an arugula salad."

"That's your go-to easy dinner," Claire says. "It's perfect every time."

"Yeah, and you can eat it hot or cold. That's why I made it. Anyhow, I let the insult slide because, like I said, I had a hankerin' for a little mischief—but then the sex didn't work. All he wanted to do was play motorboat."

Claire's confused. "Motorboat?"

"Yeah, he put his face between my breasts and went brrrrrrrrr, like a motorboat."

"That was his opening move?" Stanley asks, incredulous.

In an effort to stifle her laugh, Claire snorts. When all heads turn to look at her, she says, "You've never talked about mischief before. It seems odd."

"I know you think because I married young I don't have much life experience. But you can learn to do just about anything from books—even sex. And my husband was a really fun guy."

She turns. "For example, Stan, I've heard your sex on the beach story. I know exactly the place you're talking about, and while you regret **not** having had sex there, my husband and I did, many times."

She turns again. "And Claire, you regret passing up a chance to strip on stage. I know what it's like to be on

95

stage, near naked. I was a background exotic dancer in a few movies. I'm not a child. I didn't mention either of those things because I didn't want to hurt your feelings."

Claire is chastened. "I didn't mean to sound as if I was talking down..."

"I know, but you did. Don't go thinking just because you've been with more people you know everything about sex and fun."

"So, what happened after the motorboat?" Phyllis says.

"Nothing." Ronnie sighs. "The motorboat went on and on with him making small contented sounds between brrrrrrrrs. Then he started moving around, I think he was handling himself. He wouldn't accept direction or even participation from me. It was as if I was a blow-up sex doll. It was so awful, I started laughing. That broke his mood. I slipped away from him and out of bed. He started to say something, but I put my hand up and stopped him. Then I dressed, got my stuff, and left."

Her friends stare.

"I feel like such a fool. I was settling for someone with little to offer and he has the nerve to criticize me. Then he can't even..." Ronnie gestures with her hands. "I was willing to settle just to feel..."

"Cared for?" Stanley says.

"Wanted?" Claire says.

"Loved?" Phyllis says.

"I'm impressed that you got out fast and don't blame yourself," Claire says.

Ronnie looks perplexed. "Sex is something people do together. No one would just lie there and let someone use them. Would they?"

The silence that follows is broken by Claire saying, "Now, tell us about the dancing."

Ronnie is back to her old self. "I was visiting my husband on a movie set—you know, he worked in that business. The director decided he wanted one more dancer. He was a jerk and throwing a hissy fit. He spotted me and yelled, she'll do. I thought, *what the heck? If we can get this shoot done fast we can still get to the restaurant before it closes.* Then it turned out that the way I moved looked good on camera so I was asked to do a couple other films."

Claire was rapt. "What was it like?"

"Exciting, and then boring. I was glad I didn't have to perform for a living."

"And the sex on the beach," Stanley says. "Tell us about the sex on the beach."

"Ohhhh, that never got boring."

Later, on her way home, Claire wonders who else she's underestimated.

Desert Seasons-1

whole neighborhoods
of vacation homes
bake in the summer sun
empty   but not dormant

trusty sprinkler systems
nourish thirsty trees
so there will be lemons
and grapefruit in the fall

air conditioning runs
protecting furniture
covered in dust cloths
from the heat

in each empty house
a packed freezer and
a stocked wine cooler
hum   ready for a party

the dwellings entertain
a parade of caretakers
who visit and tend
to their every need

locals watch and wait
for the final flurry of activity
that signals the snowbirds
are on their way

Snowbirds Return

Claire and her friends liked not having tourists around during the pandemic. Their absence allowed the year-rounders to share a casual sense of community. But with COVID concerns waning, the snowbirds are returning to their resort town. Claire, Ronnie, Phyllis and Stanley meet to share a picnic lunch by the pool before their complex fills with seasonal visitors and all the tables are taken, leaving no room for them.

This will be Phyllis's first full season having the tourists around.

Though it's barely begun, she already has stories to tell.

"It sure changes when they come," she says. "The traffic is awful, so many people are lost and driving crazy. They're rude. I was at Trader Joe's and a woman pushed me out of her way. No, *sorry* or anything. She literally pushed me aside, moved into my spot, and stood there looking at cheeses."

"They're worse at Whole Foods," Stanley says.

Phyllis isn't done. "She was extremely skinny, and looked rickety—I was surprised she didn't click when she walked. The skin on her face was tight, like a mummy, and she wore a lot of makeup."

"They're worse at Whole Foods," Claire says.

"Much worse," Ronnie says. "And their parking lot is too small."

"Did you meet the redhead who lives across the street from you?" Stanley says.

Phyllis's voice grows louder.

"I introduced myself to her. She gave me the once over and told me Nordstrom's carries a line of clothes especially made to flatter full-figured women—she said she'd get the name for me. Who says something like that to someone they just met?"

Now, Phyllis is on a tear.

"The dog park is like a minefield. A couple days ago there were women there who I hadn't seen before. We didn't exchange so much as a howdy-doo before one of them told me she had a four-bedroom house in Olympia, Washington and a cabin near Sequim Bay. Another woman heard her and said she had a five-bedroom house in Eugene, Oregon and a cabin near Lake Tahoe.

"Then they asked me where my real home was. When I told them I live here, they walked away without saying another word. And they didn't pick up after their dogs!"

Phyllis stops long enough to take a breath but isn't finished.

"Then a woman who'd heard us talking walked up and told me that the people who live here year-round should be ashamed of themselves. That we don't do anything to contribute to the community. I asked her what she did, and she said she attended all the Ladies Club lunches, the morning coffee klatches and helped set up bingo—once."

Stanley, Claire and Ronnie take turns calming and reassuring Phyllis.

They tell her many of the seasonal people are nice. That the Canadians are great organizers and when they arrive they'll start up activities. That once the seasonal people are occupied with games and parties they'll leave the year-rounders alone.

They tell her the busybodies will talk about them behind their backs, complaining that they don't participate. But if they do participate, they'll complain about that. That's just how they are.

As predicted, after the Canadians arrive, the seasonal residents settle into vacation mode, ignoring the year-rounders, who return the favor.

The snowbirds get homesick after a few months and there is a general exodus when the temperature hits eighty-five two days in a row.

By the end of the season Phyllis has become quite fond of her up-stairs neighbors who are nice, friend-ly and funny. They even joined the women for cocktails, bringing cheese, crackers and jokes. Phyllis swapped recipes, and books with them. As much as she likes them, she's happy not to have someone in the unit above hers and glad when the season ends.

Desert Seasons-2

the snowbirds come here in the fall
from places that get cold
no expense is spared
to make them feel at home

all the desert dust
is carefully swept away
sturdy desert grass is scraped
rye* planted in its place

bushes and trees are trimmed
in a most unnatural way
water-loving annuals planted
to enhance the visitors stay

in the spring they leave
thinking the desert's green
the natural wonders of the place
they likely have not seen

*In some California desert communities that cater to seasonal residents, the draught-tolerant perennial grass is scraped and the area over-seeded with an annual rye grass that is softer and greener than the perennial. The over seed-ing process uses a lot of water and weakens the perennial base.

Restless

Claire feels discontented. Thinking she just needs to get away for a few days, she takes a trip up the California coast to Big Sur. It seems to work. She feels great during her drive home. But then, as the gate to her community slides open, she feels revulsion. She doesn't want to be here.

She tells herself there's nothing wrong with where she lives. It is the best location, in the middle of everything. She has a unit that is set up just to her liking in a complex that is beautiful. She has good friends. The surrounding communities have all the services and diversions a person could ask for: an array of great restaurants and stores; a highly rated medical system; a gorgeous library with an impressive lineup of speakers and events. Sure, her condo board is shady, but a lot of them are.

Wanting to move seems so unreasonable she hasn't mentioned it to anyone. But while hosting happy hour, she tells her friends, she doesn't intend to, it slips out.

"I've been looking at property," Claire says. "Every morning I look at the real estate listings. That's why I took that trip, I thought I just needed to be away for a while, that I'd be happy when I got back. But I'm not."

"I started looking a while ago," Ronnie says. "Our prices are up. We can get more for our money in other places."

"Me too," Phyllis says. "I feel foolish because I'm so new and this is such a great place. But it's like being caretaker of a resort. I like my neighbors and some of the other seasonal people. But I want to live in a real community."

"I thought I was the only one," Stanley says. "I noticed the difference when I was visiting with my sister. Most of the people around her live there, it's their home. It felt nice to be around people who were at home, even though I didn't share their politics."

"It's nuts to move, we live in the perfect place," Claire says.

There is a chorus of, "I knows," on Claire's upstairs patio and a "yoo-hoo, we're on our way up," from the sidewalk below.

Looking over the rail, the women see Maudine and Vance.

"We have bubbly and a proposition," Maudine says, holding up bottles of Prosecco.

Claire goes into the kitchen for glasses and an ice bucket. In short order all are seated and enjoying their drinks.

"So, what brings you here bearing bottles of bubbly?" Claire says.

"We're thinking of moving," Maudine says. "We hate that we need to leave every winter."

"We are too!" Ronnie says.

Maudine's eyes are big. "Really?"

"Yeah," Claire says. "Before you got here, we'd just admitted to each other that we've been checking real estate listings for at least the past few months."

"Oh, this is too good," Maudine says. "While we were on vacation, Vance and I met a woman who told us about a place next door to her, near Joshua Tree. It's fifty acres. For decades it was a vibrant commune. But within the past few years two members died and others moved so they could to be with family or get specialized care. Only two members remain and they're ready to talk about selling. The property has ten cottages spread around it and a large building in the middle they used as a community center. It's funky and interesting. Would you consider moving to a place like that?"

Having been looking at property, the women are ready with questions.

"Water?"

"Functioning well on site, city water along the southern property line."

"How bad are the cottages?"

"They're tired looking but structurally sound and an architectural delight. There are sculptures made from tires, bottle walls, all sorts of amazing stuff. "

"How big are they?"

"They range from seven hundred to fifteen-hundred square feet."

"What's the weather like in Joshua Tree?"

"Cooler than here. They often get a bit of snow in the winter, it usually melts within a few hours."

"When can we see it?"

"Tomorrow afternoon or Saturday morning."

"Tomorrow."

"Tomorrow."

"Tomorrow."

Vance takes out his phone. The appointment is made and the women drink a toast to their trip to Joshua Tree.

"I'll drive," Stanley says. "My truck-thing is very comfortable."

About the Author

Rose Baldwin

Like her character Claire, Rose Baldwin moved to the California desert from Wisconsin after retiring. She also became very restless during the pandemic.

This is Baldwin's third collection of connected short stories featuring Claire Wilson and her friends. *The Claire Stories* was published in 2016 and *Claire Streaking Through the Autumn of Her Life* in 2021. Her novel *Mike's Magic Burger* was published in 2017.